This is Leo.

Leo is quiet.

He likes to read in quiet. Play games in quiet.

Even dance in quiet.

He likes to talk to his mom and dad, Papa,
Grandmommy, and Tulip . . .

But Leo likes to be quiet with everyone else.

Today, Leo is worrying about his first day of
kindergarten.

Why is Leo worried? Because a letter just
arrived from his new teacher!

Dedicated
to everyone who
has found kindness
in the smallest places.

Who shares their kindness with others.

Who knows that kindness is not only
to do good, it is to do what is right. —V.A.

For my mom, Julia, who taught me everything about kindness —J.C.

Visit us on the Web! rhcbooks.com

Educators and librarians, for a variety of teaching tools,
visit us at RHTeachersLibrarians.com

Library of Congress Cataloging-in-Publication Data
is available upon request.
ISBN 978-0-593-48462-3 (trade)
ISBN 978-0-593-48463-0 (lib. bdg.)
ISBN 978-0-593-48464-7 (ebook)

The illustrations were painted digitally.

The text of this book is set
in 15-point Quasimoda.
Interior design by Rachael Cole

MANUFACTURED IN CHINA
10 9 8 7 6 5 4 3 2 1
First Edition

KINDERGARTEN

where kindness matters every day

Dear Leo,

My name is Ms. Perry.

I will be your KINDergarten teacher this year!

On our first day, we will talk about how we are going to make our kindergarten into a KINDergarten, so please come ready to share some ways you know how to be kind!

This year will be filled with new and exciting adventures. We will learn so much together.

I can't wait to meet you!

Love,

Your Teacher

RANDOM HOUSE STUDIO 🏠 NEW YORK

For the next two weeks, Leo thinks about Ms. Perry's letter every day. "I don't want new and exciting adventures," he says to his dad.

"What do *I* know about kindness?" he asks Tulip.

"I don't want to share anything with a new class," he whispers to Grandmommy.

On the first day of school, Ms. Perry greets Leo with a smile.
"Welcome, Leo!" she says. "Are you ready for your first day
of kindergarten?"

Leo's heart goes *ba-boom, ba-boom, ba-boom!* But he nods. And then he whispers, "I'm not sure."

"I understand how you feel, Leo. Any time we do something new, it can feel scary," Ms. Perry says. "Let's make a plan. If you feel worried, just let me know! We can figure out what to do together. Now, let's go into the classroom and I'll introduce you to a new friend."

Leo already likes Ms. Perry. But he still feels worried.

"Leo, meet LaNesha!" Ms. Perry says.

"Hi!" LaNesha says, looking up from a city she has been
building out of blocks. But just as she looks up . . . CRASH!

"Oh, no!" LaNesha says. The sound of the crash is loud. Leo wants to run to a safe, quiet corner of the room. But instead, he makes himself stay right where he is, helping LaNesha pick up the scattered pieces.

As LaNesha and Leo finish cleaning up the blocks, Ms. Perry calls the students to join her on the carpet.

"Hello again, everybody!" says Ms. Perry. "Let's start by talking about the letter I sent to each of you. Today we are going to make a Kindness Pledge! We'll write down the different things we can do to make our kindergarten classroom a KINDergarten. Who wants to start?"

Leo feels nervous. What if Ms. Perry calls on him?
Luckily, she calls on Juan.

"I raised my hand to share! I think that's a way to be
kind!" Juan is half-joking, half-serious. Everyone giggles.

"You are right, Juan!" Ms. Perry smiles. "It's kind to raise our hands before sharing."

A girl in the front is bouncing up and down.

"Yes, Chelsea?"

"I say nice words to my friends! Like 'please' and 'thank you.' Or 'I love the way you drew that cat!'"

"Nice words are the best words!" agrees Ms. Perry. "Let's add that to our pledge!"

After adding a few more ideas to the
Kindness Pledge, Ms. Perry announces,
"It's time to move our bodies. Let's take
a tour of the school. And remember as we
explore to keep looking for ways to be kind
so we can add them to our Kindness Pledge!"

The first stop is a small office. Leo likes
Nurse Melissa's round face and big smile.

LIBRARY

Right next door is the library.

When Leo sees a whole row of books about space,
his heart does a happy dance. He loves planets!

Leo wonders where they'll go next.

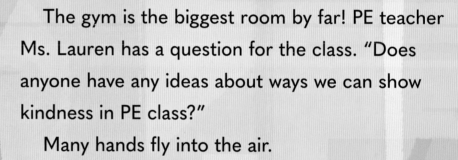

The gym is the biggest room by far! PE teacher
Ms. Lauren has a question for the class. "Does
anyone have any ideas about ways we can show
kindness in PE class?"

Many hands fly into the air.

"It's kind to ask others to play with you!" cheers Reynaldo.

"It's kind to not leave anyone out," Hena chimes in.

"If you see someone fall down, help them up!" suggests Naomi.

"Those are excellent ideas," says Ms. Perry. "Let's go back to the classroom and add them to our Kindness Pledge!"

After lunch, the class heads outside for recess. On the way, Leo nearly trips. *Oh, no,* he thinks, looking down. *How can I be ready for kindergarten when I don't even know how to tie my own shoes?*

Just then, Ms. Perry appears at his side. "May I?" She bends down to fix his laces and speaks to him softly. "Leo," she says, "I know you will have fun at recess. But sometimes it can get noisy out there. Could I introduce you to a few friends who I think you'll have fun with?"

Leo nods.

Ms. Perry introduces Leo to Mason, Marcus, and Emmie. The new friends say hello, and Marcus offers Leo some chalk.

After recess comes art class. Ms. Page greets the students. "Welcome to the studio, friends! Today you will draw pictures to decorate your Kindness Pledge. Please feel free to use any of the materials."

Leo's classmates spread out and get straight to work. But Leo isn't sure where to sit or what to create. At home, he loves to draw. (He even knows how to draw the entire solar system!) But kindness? He's not sure how to draw that.

When the students get back to the classroom, Ms. Perry says, "Our Kindness Pledge is looking great. But before we leave for the day, let's add a few more. Did you see any examples of kindness today?"

KINDNESS PLEDGE

- RAISE A HAND TO SHARE.
- USE KIND WORDS.
- STAY IN YOUR OWN BODY SPACE.
- TAKE TURNS.
- INCLUDE OTHERS WHEN WE PLAY.
- REMEMBER WE DON'T SAY, "YOU CAN'T PLAY."
- IF SOMEONE FALLS DOWN, HELP THEM BACK UP.
- SAY SORRY WHEN YOU MAKE A MISTAKE.

Lucy speaks first. "Can we add 'cleaning up our mess' to the list?" she asks. "I think that's important."

"Yes, very good, Lucy. Anyone else? What else did you see?" Ms. Perry scans the room. Leo shuts his eyes, hoping it will make him invisible.

Xochitl raises her hand. "I liked it when Ms. Page apologized for saying my name wrong. She said she's going to practice and get it right next time!"

Phew, Leo thinks as Ms. Perry calls on LaNesha. But then he hears his name.

Leo helped me pick up my block pieces this morning after my city tumbled down! That was kind.

Leo opens his eyes. More hands rise into the air.

I saw Leo picking up a bandage wrapper when we went to the nurse's office.

Leo stands in wonder.

"Leo!" Ms. Perry proclaims. "You really know how to be kind in kindergarten! And it's a good reminder that kindness isn't just in the words we say—it's also in what we do."

Leo can't believe his ears. While his heart makes the same *ba-boom, ba-boom, ba-boom*, he feels something else too. *This* must be what it feels like to be ready for kindergarten.

At dismissal, Ms. Perry says goodbye to each student one by one. She has so many ways to say goodbye! She gives smiles, fist bumps, and even high fives. She also thanks each student for helping to make the Kindness Pledge—and for being kind.

When it's Leo's turn, he has something to say even before Ms. Perry can speak. "Thank *you* for being kind, Ms. Perry! See you tomorrow!"

This is Leo on the second day of KINDergarten.
Sometimes he is still quiet.
But sometimes he isn't!
And no matter what, he is *always* kind.

KINDNESS PLEDGE

- RAISE A HAND TO SHARE.
- USE KIND WORDS.
- STAY IN YOUR OWN BODY SPACE.
- TAKE TURNS.
- INCLUDE OTHERS WHEN WE PLAY.
- REMEMBER WE DON'T SAY, "YOU CAN'T PLAY."
- IF SOMEONE FALLS DOWN, HELP THEM BACK UP.
- SAY SORRY WHEN WE MAKE A MISTAKE.
- HELP OTHERS WHEN THEY ARE HURT.
- CLEAN UP OUR MESS.
- HELP OTHERS CLEAN UP.
- HOLD THE DOOR OPEN FOR OTHERS.
- BE READY TO HELP WHEN A FRIEND NEEDS IT.
- THINK ABOUT OTHER PEOPLE'S FEELINGS.

AUTHOR'S NOTE

In this story, Ms. Perry asks the students to come up with ways to be kind for the Kindness Pledge. Having the children involved in making the pledge gives the whole class ownership over the ideas expressed in it.

Whether the poster is for a classroom or home, it can be referred to over and over again. As a teacher, I find the Kindness Pledge particularly helpful in the first few weeks of school, but all through the year there are opportunities to revisit it.

HERE ARE A FEW TIMES I'VE FOUND IT HELPFUL:

- When new visitors come or when new students join the classroom

- Before traveling to an unfamiliar place

- When a new situation/experience arises (learning something new, playing a new game, or trying new food)

- When there is a conflict

- When you are looking to spread a little joy

- When upsetting things happen in your community or the world

- After a long break or holiday and you want to get your return off to a great start

I also like to remind my students that kindness starts with being good to yourself. With so much emphasis on being kind to our classmates, sometimes they forget that. Helping children not become frustrated when they make a mistake, or simply encouraging them to be the special and unique individuals they are, is a step toward self-kindness. Kindness is more than an act—it's an attitude. And that starts with how we speak to ourselves in the mirror.